This book belongs to:

_____

For my Mama x

Books in the series...

Written by Katie Lorna McMillan
Illustrated by Graeme Andrew Clark
First printing 2017
ISBN 978-1-9997427-8-2
Published by Laughing Monkey Publishing

www.laughingmonkeypublishing.co.uk
email — info@laughingmonkeypublishing.co.uk

Find us on Facebook at
Haggis MacDougall — The mouse with a very long tail

For more illustrations by Graeme Andrew Clark,
visit - www.oldmangrey.com

Printed in Scotland

Haggis MacDougall
Saves the Day

Written by Katie Lorna McMillan
Illustrated by Graeme Andrew Clark

To Anna,
Love
Katie x

My name is Haggis MacDougall. I have a very long tail for a mouse.

It helps me on my adventures every time I leave the house.

My tail used to drive me mad and make me very sad,

But now I think it is wonderful and makes me really glad.

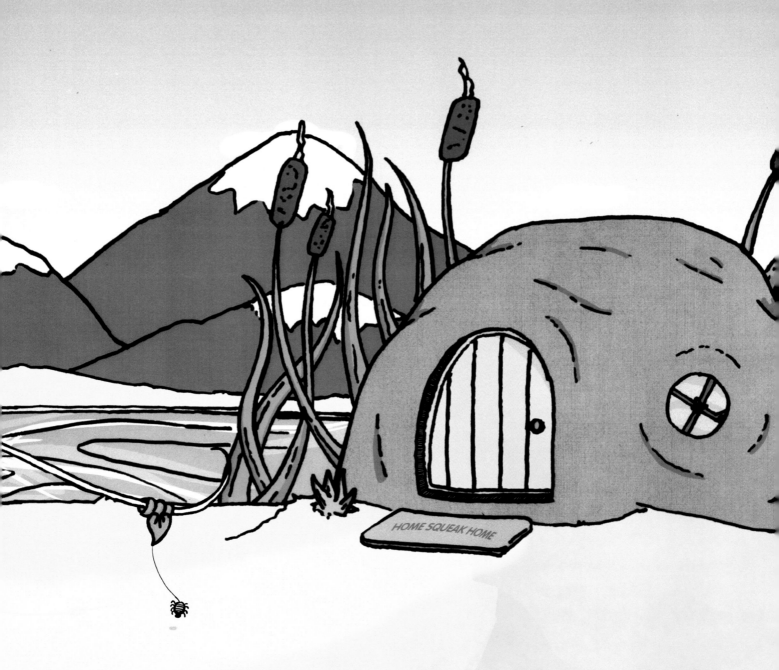

So, here is my new story
that I can't wait to tell,

About a little blue rabbit
who fell down a well.

Baxter is the name of this
little blue bunny,

Who was playing near the well
as he thought it would be funny.

So...

I peered down the well when I heard some small cries

And saw a blue bunny with tears in his eyes.

"Help me!" said Baxter, "I'm stuck in this well.

I was playing hopscotch and my foot slipped and fell."

"I shouldn't have been here,
my mama told me so.

This well is so dangerous
and I'm never allowed to go."

"So I snuck out my burrow and hopped up to the well.

I wanted to be daring, but then I slipped and fell."

"My paws are really sore
and I think I have grazed my knee.

I fell so quick and it's dark
down here and I find it hard to see.

I feel a little scared and I'm so glad
you are here.

Haggis MacDougall, my dear friend,
please take away my fear."

So I said...

"Oh, silly little Baxter, you should listen to your mummy.

You know she loves you very much. She wouldn't find this funny.

Let me go and get some help before she starts to worry.

I promise to be very quick, I know you're in a hurry."

I scurry down the road and I spy Baxter's older brother.

"Please help me Buddy, but do not tell your mother!"

"What's going on," said Buddy, "is wee Baxter ok?"

"Yes, he's fine, but a little bit stuck, that's all I can really say."

So Buddy said...

"I always worry about my brother, he loves to run away.

I don't understand why he can't just listen and stay in our garden to play.

Poor Mama will be so upset if he isn't home for tea.

Thank you Haggis for thinking so fast and asking for help from me."

Arriving at the well, Buddy shouts down to his brother,

"I am here to try and help you because you can't upset our mother."

"Please just get me out of here, I'm tired, hungry and cold!

Please send your tail down to me and I will take ahold."

Buddy holds me tightly so I don't fall down too.

He is pretty strong for a rabbit and clings to me like glue.

"Don't worry Baxter, help is here, I'm sending down my tail.

It is very long and very strong and certainly not frail."

My long, long tail swooshes down the well and lands at Baxter's feet.

He holds on tight and climbs up fast until our faces finally meet.

"Hooray, hooray I'm free at last,
your tail is truly great!

It has saved my life and helped me out
of a very sorry state."

"I promise not to run away or play where it's not safe to go.

I promise to always listen when Mama says please go slow.

I didn't think I would get hurt, but it looks like I was wrong.

Your tail is truly great and you're lucky it is so long."

So now this story is over and Baxter knows he made a mistake.

It is important to listen to Mama's advise on what roads are safe to take.

You may get lost or hurt yourself and even end up sad,

So always think before you run and you will always be glad you had.

 **The Haggis Quiz**

1. What colour is Baxter the rabbit?

2. Where is Baxter when Haggis finds him?

3. How did he end up at the bottom of a well?

4. Who did Haggis find to help him pull Baxter out of the well?

5. Who told Baxter to stay away from the well?

6. Did Haggis and his tail save the day?

7. Did you see the spider on some of the pages? If not, have a look through the book and see how many spiders you can find.

For the answers to this quiz and more Haggis activities, please visit **www.laughingmonkeypublishing.co.uk**